Randy, Cactus & Uncle Ed

The Story of the Golden Age of Louisville Television

Randy, Cactus & Uncle Ed

The Story of
the Golden Age
of Louisville
Television

David Inman

REGENCY
BOOKS

Published by:
Regency Books, Inc and David Inman
10344 Bluegrass Parkway
Louisville, KY 40299

ISBN 0-9705861-1-6

Printed in the United States of America

To Nora and Sam,
Who know all the words to the "T-Bar-V Ranch" theme song;

And to Becky,
Who understands why I wanted to teach it to them.

INTRODUCTION

This is a book about something that doesn't exist anymore – homegrown television produced by hometown talent.

In the early days of television, from roughly 1948 to, say, the 1960s, in cities across the country, there was lots of airtime to fill and precious little network programming to fill it. Into this void stepped singing cowboys, radio deejays, teenage dancers, and clowns. And, possibly, you.

In Louisville, if you were a Boy or Girl Scout, you and your troop might have appeared on "Hayloft Hoedown," waving at the camera and telling riddles to the show's comedy relief, "Cactus" Tom Brooks. If you were a teenager, you might have appeared on "Al Henderson's Dance Party" or "Teen Beat" or "Hi Varieties" doing the twist or playing "Too Fat Polka" on your accordion. If you were an adult, you might have been interviewed on "Small Talk," "Good Living" or "The Morning Show." You might

Bill Gladden was among the early cadre of television announcers who worked live, with hand-held microphones, painted backdrops and cameras up close and personal.

Randy Atcher and Judy Marshall on "Hayloft Hoedown" in the mid-1960s.

have appeared as a contestant on a locally produced game show like "Guess Who" or "Walton Calling." And, of course, if it was your birthday, you might have appeared on "T-Bar-V Ranch."

Local TV made stars of the people who hosted or performed on these shows – Randy Atcher, Phyllis Knight, Bob Kay and Livingston Gilbert, among many others. It gave the rest of us a chance to be stars in our neighborhoods, if just for a day or so. Long before the term was coined, local TV was interactive, offering access to practically everyone in the community who had a good story to tell, a song to sing or a birthday to celebrate. In the mid-1950s, African Americans were still segregated in Louisville movie theaters and lunch counters, but they could appear with Randy and Cactus on "T-Bar-V Ranch" or audition for King or Queen of the WHAS Crusade for Children on "Hi Variet-

ies." Muhammad Ali's boxing career began on WAVE's "Tomorrow's Champions."

Local television stations still exist, of course, but except for news, local programming really doesn't exist any more. For a long time now it has been cheaper to run syndicated programming, which is why today you see the same shows whether you're in Los Angeles, Lubbock or Louisville. Thirty-five years ago you got a sense of an individual city, its tastes and local talent, from its TV programming. Today, no matter where you go, it's all Oprah and Jerry Springer and "Entertainment Tonight".

To add insult to injury, most of local TV was produced in the days before cheap, accessible videotape, so most of it is gone.

Except in memories, which you will find here.

And those memories, along with pictures, were graciously contributed by Randy Atcher, Bob Bowman, Sam Gifford, Louise and Ryan Halloran, David Jones, Mike Kallay, Bob Kay, Phyllis Knight, Sleepy Marlin, Milton Metz, Ray Moran, Monnie Walton Parker, Bob Pilkington, Jerry Rice, Kaelin Kallay Rybak, Julie Shaw and Ray Shelton. It was a delight to hear their experiences and an honor to chronicle their stories. Every effort has been made to recount the atmosphere of their time, and provide information about shows on which they appeared. Any sins of commission or omission are the fault of the author and no one else.

Bill Butler helped in shaping the book and choosing photos. He and his Regency Books partner, Chris Shaw, designed and produced the book. Bob Fulbright of WAVE is the station's archivist by default, rescuing dozens of historic photos and negatives from the fate of the dumpster. His sole motivation is a love of the station's history, and without his work this book would have suffered. Ray Shelton generously provided access to audio tapes he made of WHAS personalities, including the late "Cactus" Tom Brooks, sharing their memories. David Jones passed on some audio and video tapes of WHAS-TV programs that were extremely helpful. As always, my wife, Rebecca Terry, and children, Sam and Nora Inman, provided love and support. My friend Cary Stemle at the *Louisville Eccentric Observer* helped get the ball rolling by commissioning a story about "T-Bar-V Ranch." Many people from around the area sent me their stories and photos from those days, a testament to the power of these memories and the lasting impact of the shows.

When I first began working at *The Louisville Times* in 1981, I would get the strangest feeling of *deja vu* every time I walked past a freight elevator just outside the news room. It took me a few weeks to realize that was the same freight elevator I had been herded into with a couple of dozen other kids to attend a "T-Bar-V Ranch" broadcast back in 1962 or '63. (In those days, WHAS-TV was in the same building as the newspapers.) Sometimes I still step into that freight elevator and take a ride for old times' sake.

Here's hoping this book of memories gives you the same feeling.

Contents

CHAPTER 1
Radio with Pictures—
WAVE-TV Goes on the Air

On Wednesday, November 24, 1948, Huber's Bar at 26th and Duncan changed its name to Huber's Television Bar.

Bensinger's Furniture Store on West Market was advertising the Admiral "Magic Mirror" Television for only $329.95, plus installation.

Louisville Radio and Refrigerator Sales on West Chestnut invited patrons to drop in at 8 p.m. and see something totally new to the city:

Television.

At 8 p.m., WAVE-TV went on the air from its studios at Preston and Broadway. It was the state's first television station and made Louisville the 22nd city to begin regularly scheduled television programs. There were about 2,000 televisions in Louisville, many of them installed by a team of experts – someone from the store where the set was purchased, from the factory and from WAVE itself – to ensure the best reception.

Left: Veteran WAVE-TV announcer and news anchor Livingston Gilbert introduces a program in the early 1950s.

Longtime WAVE producer-director Burt Blackwell (standing, in necktie) directs an early WAVE-TV program.

On that night virtually all 2,000 of them were tuned to channel 5, WAVE's frequency until 1953, when the FCC approved WAVE's move to channel 3 and WHAS's move from channel 9 to 11 – part of an FCC reallocation that moved channels 5 and 9 to Cincinnati.

Announcer Burt Blackwell, an announcer who also signed WAVE radio on the air in 1933, emceed the two-hour TV show, which included a film history of Louisville "from oxcart to television." Students of the Lilias Courtney Dance School presented a ballet. Bob Reed and Mary Ann Miller offered songs. Clayton "Pappy" McMitchen and his Georgia Wildcats provided instrumental music. Bea Davidson did a comic lip-synch to a Jo Stafford record. O.B. Carpenter did some hillbilly humor. Mayor Charles Farnsley congratulated WAVE president George Norton Jr. on the station's debut.

Also playing roles on the broadcast were WAVE announcers Livingston Gilbert, Bill Gladden, Ryan Halloran, Ed Kallay and Bob Kay. All but one would spend their entire careers at the station – Gladden, after being the station's commercial spokesman for Greater Louisville First Federal Savings and Loan, would leave WAVE in 1971 and work full time for the bank until his death in 1975.

When WAVE-TV moved from channel 5 to channel 3 on the dial in 1953, Ed Kallay was there with a map to explain the station's increased coverage as a result of the change.

In the days before videotape, TV newscasts relied on maps and still pictures to tell stories, as in this shot from the late 1950s with WAVE announcer Ryan Halloran.

Watching from their West End home were Ed Kallay's family, including son Mike.

"We were the first kids on the block to have a TV set, and we had a good reason for it," Kallay recalled. "The box was the size of an enormous mainframe computer and the screen was the size of a saucer."

The inaugural show wasn't exactly free of problems. One sponsor had a large display of crystal glassware on a drop-leaf table that, at some point during the broadcast, dropped a leaf.

And Ryan Halloran's wife Louise remembers the ballet getting a mixed reception.

"Some man called the station and asked where the studio was, on the first or second floor," she recalled. "They told him the second floor and he said, 'Good, just have the ballet dancer leap out the window.'"

For more than a year, WAVE's programming was almost all local, all the time.

Network programs directly from NBC weren't available because the nationwide coaxial cable didn't yet make a stop in Louisville. Some NBC programs were available on kinescope – a filmed recording of a live program that was then shipped to stations across the country. The time lag was usually a few days at least, more often a week, but Bill Ladd, TV and Radio Editor of *The Courier-Journal*, said hopefully, "You possibly would get the inauguration of President Truman the night of the event, in time to see it all before going to bed."

Because of the lack of programs, the station's schedule was spartan – only from 7 p.m. to 10 p.m.– and at least one day a week there was nothing on at all. Exceptions were made for special events, such as the following day's Thanksgiving football game between Male and Manual high schools. (In 1948 Manual won, 14-0.)

That first week on the air, WAVE's Friday night program lineup included "Fort Knox Passin' Review" and a movie. A hockey game was broadcast on Saturday, with the Louisville Blades taking on Detroit. Sunday included a kinescope of the NBC program "Philco TV Playhouse." On Monday came "Junior's Club," a precursor of "Funny Flickers," with host Ed Kallay, ventriloquist Norma Jarboe and Junior, a pop-eyed dummy in a houndstooth jacket. Tuesday's programming included wrestling matches sponsored by Fehr's Beer.

Almost everything was live. There was no tape delay – no tape at all, for that matter. "Really we didn't know what to do with it at first," said Kay, who was with WAVE from 1941 to 1982. "Then again, neither did anybody else."

"We were very curious about it, excited to be part of it," said Halloran, with WAVE from 1946 to 1985. "But we didn't quit our radio jobs."

Halloran's first show on WAVE-TV was a video version of his radio show, "Dialing for Discs." (Later the format grew to include film footage, and the name was changed to "Platters and Pix.")

Ryan Halloran came to WAVE-TV from WAVE radio, and on "Dialing for Disks" he played records for the TV audience.

Bob Kay once made a guest appearance with Halloran and experienced the heat of live television firsthand. "We had those hot lights, really hot," Kay recalled. "The perspiration just ran down your face. I always tell people that Ryan really grilled me that day."

As the staff expertise grew, so did the daily schedule, and the workload.

"Everything had to be done live – the commercials, the station breaks, the shows," said Ray Moran, an engineer with WAVE from 1951-91. "It was like putting on a stage show all day long. We had a very large staff – engineers, announcers, a full production crew including a prop department and carpenters. There was always action, all the time."

Ed Kallay stands at the "Magic Gateway", part of a short-lived weekend version of his daily "Magic Forest" TV series, in 1954.

Corn, anyone? Rodney Ford (in rocking chair) as "Burley Birchbark" in a 1954 photo. Bob Kay stands next to him.

"Pop the Question" was a locally-produced game show, complete with studio audience, co-hosted by Bob Kay and Rosemary Reddens (center).

The news according to Polaroid—a WAVE camerman pans across a series of small photos in this 1954 shot; the weather map is just below.

There was "Flavor to Taste," a local cooking show hosted by Miriam Kelly; Foster Brooks' "Man on the Street" program, taking place each day on Broadway; Halloran's "Dialing for Discs"; Brooks again as "The Old Sheriff" in an afternoon children's program; Rodney Ford (later the station's news director and editorial spokesman) as "Burley Birchbark" in a weekly show of cornpone humor; "The Pee Wee King Show"; and daily audience participation shows such as "Pop the Question," "Dollar Derby" and "Ladies Fare."

Not to mention live newscasts and live, on-air commercials.

"There were no networks, no cable – you just did the news yourself," remembered Halloran. "You'd have a board that you would put a Polaroid picture onto to illustrate your stories. While camera one focused on one board, you'd put a picture on another board with camera two and you would cut to that. The word 'announcer' was a flattering term in those days. You were expected to have the skill to do everything – conduct a broadcast, do news, sports, whatever needed to be done."

Including the beer commercials. In those days, Louisville was home to at least three breweries – Oertel's, Fehr's and Falls City – which advertised on TV.

As announcer and sidekick on "The Pee Wee King Show," Kay did commercials for Oertel's '92 Beer. "At first, they wanted you to drink the beer," Kay said. "I was supposed to hold up a glass of brew and say, 'Cheer up with Oertel's '92 and get more fun out of life.' But by drinking it, it came out, 'Cheer up with Oertel's '92 and blub blub blub.' "

The union ruled out beer drinking, however, and a great premium was put on properly pouring a glass of beer so that it didn't overflow the glass or wasn't all foam.

"Finally, a man from Fehr's Beer told me, 'Halloran, either talk or pour – don't do both,' " Halloran said. "So I shut up, poured the beer and then started talking again, and that was fine with them. But the sponsor always wanted you to eat the hamburger, drink the beer, bite the cookie, whatever."

Another announcer who just couldn't memorize a commercial solved his problem by walking off camera to read the script, until one night when the cameraman followed him instead of staying focused on the product.

Other tricks were common – like the night Foster Brooks opened a refrigerator on the air and pulled

Ed Kallay reads the sports in a crowded 1954 studio that includes the "Burley Birchbark" set and a display to be used in a Reynolds Aluminum commercial.

Foster Brooks (standing, in horn-rim glasses) and his cohort zoom across the galaxy in a cardboard spaceship in this show from the mid-1950s.

out a rival sponsor's beer someone had put in as a joke. He did the whole commercial without realizing it and then, at the end of the spot, recognized the rival brand, dropped the bottle and walked off the air.

Ed Kallay was demonstrating the first canned whipped cream on the air and forgot to shake the can before squirting it, thus dousing himself and the sponsor in goo, not whipped cream.

Livingston Gilbert was so intent on reading the cue card during a beer commercial that, while pouring it, he missed the glass entirely.

Bob Kay was doing a Donaldson's bread commercial and his script line, "the best in bread" came out "the breast in bed."

Once during "Dialing for Discs" the camera focused on a pretty girl walking outside the studio just as a truck drove in front of her with a sign that said "Free Pickup."

Despite occasional bloopers, however, there was no doubt that this radio with pictures was here to stay. By 1949, WAVE engineers decided to try and bring live World Series broadcasts to Louisville. The station built an antenna on Floyds Knobs in Indiana and microwaved the signal to the studio.

The WAVE-TV doors open on square dancers in this shot from 1953.

Bob Kay hosts the Donaldson Play Club, sponsored by Donaldson's Bread, in the mid-1950s.

More network shows were on the schedule by then – from all the national networks, since WAVE was the only game in town. Popular CBS shows such as "Arthur Godfrey and His Friends," "This Is Show Business" and Ed Sullivan's "Toast of the Town" were shown on kinescopes. NBC supplied "Kukla, Fran and Ollie," "We, the People" and Perry Como's "Chesterfield Supper Club," among others, and the station ran "Cavalcade of Stars" from the DuMont network. Old Charlie Chaplin films also had a weekly spot.

More local programming was blossoming as well. "Junior's Club" became so popular on WAVE that Junior the dummy became a daily presence, hosting "Junior's Sketchbook," "Junior's Movie" and "Junior's Pet Show." Bob Kay, selling the best in bread, donned a Donaldson Bread deliveryman's uniform and hosted the "Donaldson Play Club." The station set up a camera at owner George Norton Jr.'s farm near the Oldham County line and broadcast "Farm" from there. And in May 1949, WAVE broadcast the Kentucky Derby on TV for the first time.

Audiences were growing. On "Dialing for Discs" they decided to let people call in and request songs.

"We had to stop doing that, though, because AT&T told us it was blocking the phone lines," Halloran said.

And crowds would gather every day around Foster Brooks just before he went on the air with his "Man on the Street" show. Just for fun, Brooks would convince the crowd to be totally silent and he would go on the air just moving his lips, giving soundmen back at the studio heart palpitations.

Then one day, something simple happened that vividly illustrated the power of television to the staff at WAVE-TV. It was on "Dialing for Discs." A woman whose grown daughter was recuperating in a nearby tuberculosis sanitarium called the station. It seems the woman's daughter had given birth recently, but hadn't been able to see her newborn baby since being hospitalized. But with television, she could.

"So they brought her baby into the studio and onto the show, and the mother could see this baby she couldn't see any other way," Halloran recalled. "It was a really striking example of what TV could do, and they even wrote it up in *Time* magazine."

Ray Moran, the WAVE engineer, had his own realization while visiting friends in rural Kentucky. The friend's television broke and Moran went with him to buy a replacement tube at the house of a neighbor who was a repairman.

"We looked in the front door, and we saw these two kids watching TV and an older woman sitting behind them," Moran said. "That image always stayed with me, because that was whose lives were really affected by television – the people in rural areas. It exposed them to things they'd never seen before."

From then on, they – and television – would never be the same.

The five announcers who helped WAVE-TV on the air celebrate the station's 10th anniversary in 1958– (left to right) Bill Gladden, Ed Kallay, Ryan Halloran, Livingston Gilbert and Bob Kay.

CHAPTER 2

WHAS-TV – "Black Tuesday" and Beyond

On Monday, March 27, 1950, WHAS-TV went on the air.

On Tuesday, March 28, 1950, WHAS-TV spent much of its second day on the air going off the air. They called it "Black Tuesday."

"Everyone had all worked so hard for that first day on the air, that was the focus," said announcer Ray Shelton, who was with WHAS from 1950 to 1975. "After that, everything fell apart. There was no continuity, and the story went that that day they had more black screen than they had programming."

Still, that didn't keep the station's first program from being a success.

Like WAVE-TV's first show a year and a half before, all the talent was trotted out. Bud Abbott (a longtime WHAS radio announcer, not the Abbott of Abbott and Costello) gave a comic "explanation" of television. A segment of "T-Bar-V Ranch" was introduced, featuring a just-rehired Randy Atcher (who'd been on radio station WKLO) and "Cactus" Tom Brooks. Sam Gifford previewed "Hi Varieties" and his wife, Marian Gifford, introduced "Good Living." Herbie Koch played the organ, and Bill Pickett sang. Jim Walton gave a preview of his "Walton Calling" program, an audience-participation show based on his "Coffee Call" on WHAS radio, and teamed with Roz Marquis for a preview of "Guest Book." Ken Meeker and Eloise Terry contributed bits, and newsmen and sports reporters on hand included Pete French, Dick Oberlin, Jimmy Finegan and Dick Sutterfield.

Right: Jim Walton's "Walton Calling" had it all – a prime-time slot, studio audience, silly stunts and live commercials.

PROGRAMS IN THE "BEST" TRADITION

Every night at 10:30 Ray Shelton and Kentuckiana's exclusive local newsreel. Sponsored by Greater Louisville First Federal Savings and Loan Assoc.

Every Friday at noon Lee Jordan, Allan Blankenbaker help local women have fun and prizes. Sponsored by Triangle Food Stores.

WHAS-TV Channel 9

POWER POPULARITY

Since Louisville was not yet connected to a coaxial cable, no live network programs were available. That first night, CBS network programs were shown on filmed kinescopes, including an episode of Ken Murray's variety show, "The Fred Waring Show" – headed by the bandleader and inventor of the blender – and the dramatic anthology "Studio One."

"Before the cable," said Shelton, "everything would be on a delay. Ed Sullivan's show would air on Sunday night, and then they'd put a kinescope of the show on a Greyhound bus and send it to us in Louisville."

Bob Pilkington came to WHAS-TV as a studio director – without having a real clear understanding of just what that meant. "We made our mistakes up front, in front of everybody," said Pilkington, who became the longtime producer of "Hayloft Hoedown" and was with the station from 1950 to 1988.

One announcer, doing a Pepsi commercial, held a bottle of the product up to the camera and said, enthusiastically, "Have a Coke!" Another insisted on the commercial copy being printed out and placed under the camera. "So the poor guy is reading it," said Milton Metz, who joined WHAS in 1946, "and he keeps looking down and down and down, until his eyes are looking straight down to floor level – and he's still on camera!"

One night, when he was hosting "The Late Show," Jim Walton found himself having to read the subtitles on an Italian movie because they were too far below the screen for viewers to see. Finally, at a break, Walton said, "Let's face it. The best thing to do is go to bed, folks. We've got a stinker here."

Shelton remembers doing a wristwatch commercial where the watch was frozen into an ice cube to demonstrate its ability to take a licking and keep on ticking – except that when the ice was chipped away, it was clear that the tick had been licked. "I can see

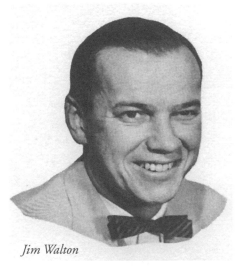

Jim Walton

the second hand isn't running," said Shelton. "And I'm supposed to hold it up to the camera so you could see that sweep second hand still moving." So he picked up the watch, swooped it in front of the camera as quickly as possible, and kept on talking.

Shelton also did commercials for the weekly "Strietmann Playhouse," an umbrella title for episodes of

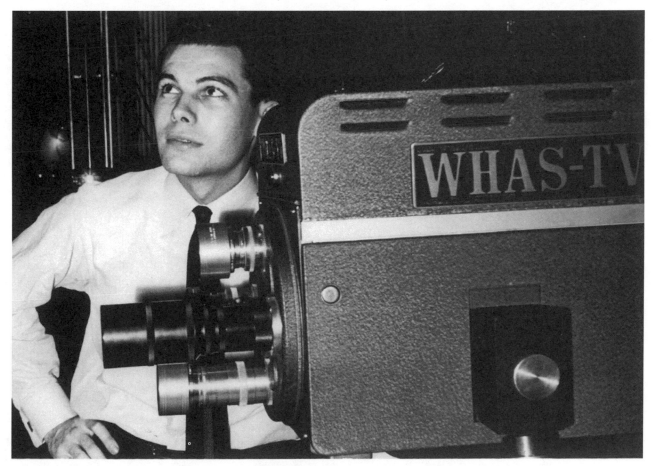

A young Ray Shelton at the WHAS studios in 1953.

"Boston Blackie" and "I Led Three Lives." Strietmann was a cookie and cracker company, and they couldn't understand why Shelton couldn't eat cookies and sell them at the same time. "They told me they had an announcer in Cincinnati who could take a big bite of a cookie, park it somewhere inside his mouth and then keep talking," Shelton said. "It sounded like he was part squirrel."

Shelton's best known commercial role, of course, was as the station's spokesman for Greater Louisville First Federal Savings and Loan, for whom he did commercials from 1950 to 1994. (He left WHAS in 1975 to work for the bank.)

"Before tape, I'd come into the station and do that spot during the 11 o'clock news every night," Shelton said. "If it was a Saturday night and we were out, I'd have to leave the party at 11 o'clock and go do that commercial."

One of Pilkington's first jobs was directing "Good Living," a daily home show done on a shoestring. "It was a cooking show, and we couldn't afford a camera to be over the stove top, so we just put a mirror there," Pilkington said. "Of course, you had to stir everything backward to make it come out all right on TV."

That challenge, however, was nothing compared to the day a steer came to visit the "Good Living" studio – on the seventh floor of *The Courier-Journal* building.

"This steer had won everything at the state fair," Pilkington said. "His name was Sleepy. They'd shot him full of something to get him into the freight elevator. They take him up to the seventh floor, and we have spread a big tarp on the floor. A guy from the stockyards was the guest, to tell where all the cuts of meat come from. I had asked him be-

fore the show went on what would happen if this massive animal decided to void its bladder. The guy said, 'Well, he kind of coughs and humps his back.' We only had two cameras, and we kept a close up for a long time just in case anything happened. But we had to go to a wide shot, and just as we did the steer kind of humped his back and cut loose. We were awash. Oh, mercy!"

Pilkington also worked with announcer Bud Abbott, who did double duty on radio and his own TV show. "Bud Abbott would try just about any-

thing," Pilkington said. He did his show practically everywhere in the Courier building, including the cafeteria and, on hot summer days, even out on the roof overlooking downtown Louisville.

"Once we talked Abbott into putting a rope around his leg and letting us hoist him into the air, so the program would open with him saying something about hanging around," Pilkington said. "When they hoisted him up, he was very uncomfortable and a little scared, so as soon as we went on the air he said, 'Hi, I'mjusthangingaroundnowletmedown!'

Bud Abbott's show featured comedy and celebrities, such as fan dancer Sally Rand.

"The Bud Abbott Show" featured parodies of commercials, such this one for an ultra king-size cigarette (above). Looking on is Milton Metz as evil Squire Snoopy McSneer. (Below) Abbott does a comic bit with a paratrooper.

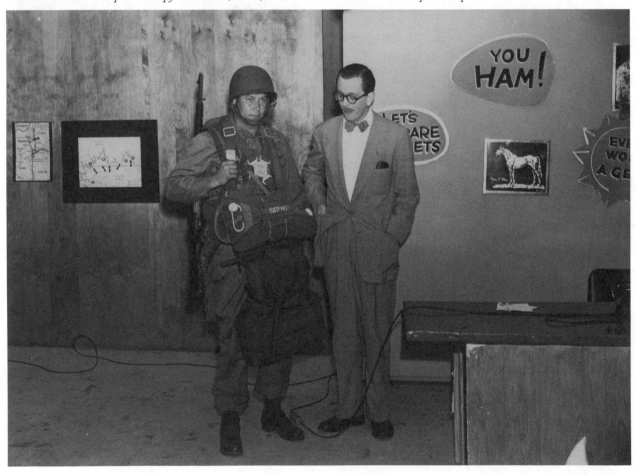

Pilkington played his own role on "The Bud Abbott Show" – in the form of comic-strip style word balloons. If Abbott would criticize Pilkington's script, the camera would cut to a sign reading "every word a gem." The show also parodied current network TV fare like the glitzy interview show "The Stork Club." In Abbott's version, Milton Metz – dressed as evil Squire Snoopy McSneer – was a guest. It was all about having fun – and not having a budget.

"Ingenuity played a great role in what we did," said Metz. His idea was to do a nightly weather forecast with a difference, and the difference was suggested by his wife Miriam. "My wife came up with the idea for the Magic Weather Writer," a device Metz used on his show. "It was a box-like thing with mirrors, and someone would write the forecast so that it seemed to appear 'magically.' Then we would use magnetic symbols for what the weather would be, and the hot and cold ex-

Milton Metz does the weather.

tremes – the nation's icebox and the oven. And we'd always tell the temperature in Caribou, Maine. It just became a kind of tradition."

Many of Metz's weather symbols included the WHAS "Fisbie" emblem, developed in 1956 by staff artist Allan Blankenbaker. Fisbie was a man whose eyes were the ones in the number eleven, and until the late 1960s he was the personification of the station. Fisbie's name was an acronym of the station's tag line – "Foremost in Service, Best in Entertainment."

By 1953, when WHAS changed from channel 9 to channel 11, the schedule included such local pro-gramming as "Lure of the Library," "Small Talk," What's Your Question?," "The Herbie Koch Show" and "Let's Look It Over."

"Walton Calling" played to packed audiences, many of whom got into the act. One woman was blind-folded and told to propose to her husband. He was ushered out and a monkey was brought in. Another time, announcer Shelton, doing commercials for sponsor Will Sales Company, was blindfolded and told to describe the curves in a refrigerator while it was replaced by a model in a swimsuit.

The show was structured to include songs by organist Johnny Schrader and singer Bill Pickett, and the result was very successful – in 1953 "Walton Calling" was among Louisville's most popular shows, drawing audiences the size of those watching "I Love Lucy" and "Dragnet."

But in 1955, after over five years on the air, "Walton Calling" was getting too expensive to produce and was getting beaten in the ratings by "Caesar's Hour" on NBC. "Walton Calling" was replaced by a filmed series from Hollywood, "Eddie Cantor's Comedy Playhouse."

It was a sign of things to come.

CHAPTER 3

Kids Shows, from Singing Cowboys to Talking Ducks

T-Bar-V Ranch.

If you're a longtime Louisvillian and you're old enough to remember when Muhammad Ali Boulevard was Walnut Street, when Dillard's was Stewart's and when a riverbat was a nocturnal animal that lived along the Ohio, then you probably know the song:

Brush your teeth each morning,
Get lots of sleep at night,
Mind your mom and daddy
'Cause they know what is right.
Lots of exercise each day
And eat up all your food,
And always wear a great big smile
That makes you look so good.
Be sure to look both left and right
Before you cross the street
And be with us tomorrow at nine
When it's T-Bar-V Ranch time!

Left: Howdy! "Cactus" Tom Brooks, Randy Atcher and Tiny Thomale welcome you to T-Bar-V Ranch.

31

Yes, it's the closing theme from "T-Bar-V Ranch," also known as the "Brush Your Teeth Song."

"T-Bar-V Ranch" ran on WHAS-TV from 1950 to 1970. In those 20 years Randy Atcher and grizzled co-host "Cactus" Tom Brooks—who died in 1997 at age 87—interviewed more than a hundred thousand children who were celebrating their birthdays on the daily show.

If it was your birthday, you'd dress up in your best cowboy outfit or prettiest dress and white gloves. You'd go downtown to WHAS-TV's studios in the Courier-Journal building at Sixth and Broadway. There, grandfatherly Bill Sheehy would take you in a freight elevator up to the sixth floor. Your parents would wait there, watching the show on a monitor, while you were taken up one more floor to the studio.

Sometime during the hour you would have your moment in the spotlight, being interviewed by

Randy or "Cac" and then waving to everybody watching at home—Mommy, Daddy, relatives, friends, enemies. "Of course the one story everybody remembers," Atcher said, "is where the little boy got up in front of the camera and hi to mommy and daddy," and then, raising his middle finger, said, "And THIS is for you, Herbie!"

Well, that's show biz.

And the story of how Atcher hooked up with "T-Bar-V Ranch" involves World War II, a "Happy Birthday" march, and Tom Brooks' brother Foster's alimony.

Born into a family of musicians, Atcher, now 82, began playing and yodeling – yes, yodeling – on local radio in the early 1930s. He went from WHAS to KMOX in St. Louis and then to a stint in Chicago with brother Bob and orchestra leader Ben Bernie's band. His popularity grew to the degree that there was talk of a screen test and a movie career similar to that of Roy Rogers and Gene Autry.

Instead, World War II came along, and Atcher enlisted in the Air Force. After the war he came back to Kentucky and to WHAS radio, then stations WGRC and WKLO.

Meanwhile, WHAS-TV was about to go on the air. One of its programs would be a video version of the popular radio show "Circle Star Ranch," hosted by cowboy singer Roy Starkey and Tom Brooks.

But there was a problem. The station brass wanted Starkey to sing "Happy Birthday" in a march tempo while the kids tromped around the T-Bar-V set. Starkey couldn't sing it that way.

"They asked me if I could sing 'Happy Birthday' to a march tempo," Atcher recalled. "I said I'd sing it in any tempo they wanted." So WHAS made an offer to Atcher, and Atcher went to his boss at WKLO.

"He said, 'Television is just a fad, it'll never last,'" Atcher said. "Foster Brooks at that time was at WKLO and I knew they were paying Foster's salary and his alimony. So I said, 'If you pay me what you're paying Foster, I'll stay.' They wouldn't do that, and it was probably the best thing that ever happened to me."

Tom Brooks originated the character of Cactus on "Circle Star Ranch." He had been hired at WHAS radio during a World War II labor shortage, with no radio background – although brother Foster, as noted, was already a local radio legend.

Tom Brooks' own announcing career had been iffy; he was affected with nerves and stammering. His boss gently suggested that he start looking for another line of work. But one day, Brooks hit on the idea of taking out his false teeth to read the role of a cowboy bumpkin on "Circle Star Ranch," and before you could say, "How-DEEE!" Cactus was born.

In real life, Brooks was a dapper dresser who sported a pencil-thin mustache. He delighted in walking unrecognized past groups of children touring the station and letting out with a trademark "How-DEEEE!" before disappearing into an office.

He also loved slipping Cactus dialect into his regular on-air announcing duties. To wit: "This is WHAS-TV, Louisville, Kentucky. The time: Seb-un Thirty."

"T-Bar-V Ranch" went on the air the day WHAS-TV went on the air—March 27, 1950. Atcher recalled, "We had children of the staff on the first show. We didn't know what to do regarding ages, so we had kids as old as 11, 12 or 13. Of course, now they're 64. After a while we narrowed it down – we found that if they were three years old they couldn't be away from mom, and above 8 they were a little cynical."

Of course, even limiting the ages didn't stop kids like the Herbie-hater from coming on. And since the show was done live, there was nothing to do but swallow hard and keep going. "We used to have special guests on the show – firemen, police officers, nurses – and it was one of those dry summers," Randy recalls. "So the fireman came on and talked to the children about making sure their parents didn't put throw their lit cigarettes out the window when they were on a drive. And he said, 'You just tell mom and dad to keep their butts in the car.' When something like that happens, you just look down and try not to laugh."

Wet pants were common. And if Randy was doing a live sales spot, he'd often have to deal with some unwanted assistance—like the time he was doing a milk commercial and a child stood next to him repeating, "I don't like milk, Randy. I don't like milk." Or the time a child told Randy on the air that he didn't watch "T-Bar-V" anymore, because, his sister chimed in, "Daddy hocked the TV set!"

"Parents like T-Bar-V almost as much as the youngsters do, because Randy and Cactus inject timely safety and health reminders into the patter of the daily shows. The extent of their influence on the kiddies can be measured by the scores of phone calls the men get during the year from parents asking them to tell Junior, over the phone, that he must drink his milk and eat his food if he's to grow up big like they are."

T-Bar-V sales sheet from the mid-1950s

The desire to impart a lesson or two was what inspired Atcher to write the show's "Brush Your Teeth Song." That, and the fact that if you played "Happy Birthday" on the air, march tempo or no, you had to pay a royalty to ASCAP.

"I knew repetition was important in writing a children's song," Atcher says. "We used the same melody as the opening theme, and it must have worked, because people still remember it."

They still remember the opening, too:

> *Howdy! Howdy! Boys and girls,*
> *it's T-Bar-V Ranch time!*
> *We're glad to see you all today*
> *and hope you're feeling fine.*
> *We'll sing and dance and have a show*
> *and birthday parties too!*
> *It's T-Bar-V Ranch time!*

And at that time the show aired at 3 p.m., so the closing line was "Be with us tomorrow at three/ When it's time for T-Bar-V."

Allan Blankenbaker's puppets were on hand, including William Harris Allen Smith Gnu. (Note the initials.) Barbara Miller, a librarian from the Louisville Free Public Library, was a frequent visitor. An Afro-American woman, she had a gentle style and kind manner that transcended color.

A coin bank was on the set, decorated with the station's "Fisbie" mascot, into which children could plunk donations for the Crusade for Children.

From almost the beginning, the influence of "T-Bar-V Ranch" was felt far and wide. One of its sponsors, Greater Louisville First Federal Savings and Loan, began a "Savings Post" campaign to get young viewers to open bank accounts. By 1956, over 20,000 kids had saved over $1 million, and the bank had built a child-sized western town, complete with old-time bank, on an upper floor of its downtown office.

That same year, in connection with another offer, Randy and Cac announced that viewers who wrote in would receive a free coloring book. More than 22,000 kids responded, and the coloring book had to go into extra printings.

As late as 1968, Randy and Cactus were still icons. An article in *The Louisville Times* reported that after Cactus signed a child's arm at a personal appearance, the child wouldn't wash it off. A week later, the child's mother phoned Cactus, who urged the child to take a bath, and promised to mail the child an autographed photo.

Those who appeared on the show have vivid memories of meeting Randy and Cactus. Emily Portman Rice remembered that a King and Queen were chosen from the children celebrating birthdays on the show.

"I was chosen queen and my brother Frank was chosen king," she said, and they each were given a crown-like hat. "I didn't know I was supposed to give the hat back. Someone took my brother's hat, but they didn't take mine, so I kept it. As we were waiting for the bus to take us home, Frank saw I was still wearing my hat and wasn't too happy about it. He had me so scared about keeping it that I was afraid to watch the show the next day. I just knew that Randy was going to go on television and say, 'Emily Portman, bring back that hat!' But the next day no one mentioned the hat. There was another king and queen. I guess they must have had more hats. And I wasn't arrested."

Ron Lewis, still a Louisville resident, poses with Randy in a 1954 photo.

Photo courtesy of Dana Boucher

"I was an only child, and my best friend was number five of six daughters," remembered another visitor, Joyce Wilson. "When my best friend's little sister wanted to go to the show, my Mom and her Mom decided we should see if all three girls could go at the same time since we were about the same age. The little sister got to go before we did. When she got home she was indeed the talk of the whole block. Even thought the little sister didn't even talk to Randy or Cactus and she cried and wouldn't even say Hi to Mommy or Daddy, she came home with a coupon for two White Castle hamburgers and a medium drink and a Jim-Jam! (Jim-Jams were the best snack cake ever, and they cost a quarter.) All I could think about was getting to go to the W.C. Lounge without my Dad grousing about money and I could get a 25-cent Jim-Jam. I was going to take my new Gene Autry lunch box with the glass lined thermos (where I kept my marble collection). The day finally came and I found myself in the studio with my dress starched way too much, my plaits as tight as inhumanly possible and my Gene Autry and Champion lunch box. (Mom nixed the marbles). As I was led to the stage I got off on a bad start. We didn't get White Castle cou-

pons; we only got a Banana Flip cake. I was despondent. Who cared now? This ordeal became worse. Cactus smelled funny (the face paint) and Randy smelled like cigarettes. Randy hurried me up and tried to make me stand on the box. I didn't want to stand on the box, but I was deposited on the dreaded box. I loudly let him know about the inequity of being gypped out of the whole reason to be on T Bar V, and Randy never knew what hit him. For good measure I also reiterated to him he was hurting me and was going to make me fall off this stupid box. It was all over so quick. I never got to show my lunch box sans the marbles. My best friend was with Cactus and she was crying too (must have run in the family). The ride home was forever long. My friend got sick on the bus. My mom was not happy with me and even my offer of a banana flip fell on her deaf ears (it finally ended up in Dad's lunch box)."

Photo courtesy of Juanita Nanz

Then there was the "cake" Cactus would bring out for the birthday party. He would bumble and stumble and pretend to fall with it, while the kids squealed. "My first great life's lesson: Discovering that the big birthday cake that Cactus pretended to almost drop every day was made of cardboard," said C.D. Kaplan. "They gave some explanation beforehand to ease the dismay of the first-time kids. I remember being so distraught and disillusioned." Mary Knight Halloran, the daughter of longtime WAVE sportscaster Joe Knight, appeared on the show "and after I'd done my birthday bit they brought me back up to ask about my dad. Then they said something about WAVE-ing to my dad, who I believe was in the WHAS studio at the time. I remember all the adults and crew laughing."

"My mom was a childhood friend of Cactus," recalled Beth McBride. "She always signed me up to

Photo courtesy of Kim Nuss

talk to him. I wanted to talk to Randy because I thought he was cute, and that painted mole on Cactus' chin scared me. Later, I was waving to everyone at home and Cactus kept asking me questions. I would answer his questions while waving."

Roger Sargent has memories of being possibly the most disruptive child on the show, which is saying something. "My twin brother and I were both on it back in the late '50s or early '60s. My mother along with the lady next door took my brother and I to the show – my two older brothers were home watching with great anticipation. According to my brothers and mom, I was seen constantly getting up and running in front of the camera trying to get to a table of cupcakes on the other side of the room. People were chasing me and trying to get me to sit down with the other children, but I would have nothing to do with it. My brother apparently kept trying to grab Randy's gun from his holster and Randy could be heard saying 'I have told you for the last time – leave my gun alone.' Apparently we were causing such pandemonium that they literally took us both by the wrist and hauled us back downstairs to the parents' room, where my horrified and embarrassed mother was sitting with her neighbor friend who was nearly on the floor in hysterical laughter."

Another sign of the show's power was felt one year at Christmas time. The show's storyline in those days involved bad guy Squire Snoopy McSneer (played by Milton Metz), who stole Santa's reindeer just before Christmas. "Squire McSneer was a very melodramatic villian," Metz recalled. "My wife had a tall girlfriend who had this great velvet cape, and I'm a hat collector, so I had a top hat. I remember one time I was on the show and I had a cap pistol in my waistband. In my zeal to pull it out it flew up into the air and over the set. So I turned to Randy and Cactus and said, 'Never mind! I'll shoot you with my finger!'

"Our boss, Vic Sholis, had four kids," Atcher recalled. "And when Squire McSneer stole those reindeer, that was really serious to them. They really

Photo courtesy of Carol Janes

were sure that Santa wasn't going to come! So Vic came in and said, 'I don't care how you do it, but get those reindeer back.' And everything worked out just in time."

Unfortunately, it was also the end of Squire McSneer. "I loved it," Metz said, "but I always kept having to get the cape dry-cleaned because my payoff was always a pie in the face."

Sholis' children also exercised some control over the programming within the show. At the beginning, "T-Bar-V Ranch" included a daily chapter from an old 1930s or '40s movie serial like "Don Winslow of the Navy." "One of the serials was called 'The Clutching Hand,' and at the beginning you would see this big hand coming to grab you," Atcher said. "Well, this scared Vic's kids, and that serial just disappeared one day – we never did get to see the end of that one."

The end of "T-Bar-V Ranch" was something that Atcher and the cast didn't see coming, either. "It was completely sudden," Atcher said. "As far as we knew, T-Bar-V was just as popular in 1970 as it had ever been." Expense was cited; it was much cheaper to put a rerun in that 9 a.m. spot. So on June 30, 1970 "T-Bar-V Ranch" was replaced by old episodes of "My Favorite Martian."

But that wasn't the end of the show. The end may never come. As long as there's an adult around who remembers the phrase "brush your teeth each morning, get lots of sleep at night," then the spirit of "T-Bar-V Ranch" lives on. Go to any Internet serch engine and type in "T-Bar-V Ranch" and you'll find dozens of Web listings about the show and the theme song.

"What amazes me," Atcher said, "is I'll hear from somebody whose sister is in California and has taught her children the song. It's all over the country. Anywhere I'll go, someone will say, 'Hey, Randy!' It happens all the time. Someone'll ask if it bothers me, and it's just the opposite. I feel so good that they remember it."

"FUNNY FLICKERS" and "GUESS WHO"

While Randy and Cactus of "T-Bar-V Ranch" had a studio full of kids, Ed Kallay of "Funny Flickers" played to the kids at home, via the camera.

He'd talk to them about eating the sponsor's product (Klarer hot dogs) for lunch and bundling up before going outside on cold days. He'd tell them to "hit the sack and take that nap." He'd sign off by saying "See you round like a doughnut!" or "So long like a hot dog!"

He'd talk to sidekick Sylvester the Duck, who spoke in taped, sped-up jargon supplied either by Kallay or Livingston Gilbert. Sylvester and the magical doll Tom Foolery lived with "Uncle Ed" in the Magic Forest, and on weekday mornings and afternoons from 1953-65, so did we.

Sylvester the Duck, Uncle Ed, and Tom Foolery.

Kallay had guest sidekicks from time to time. Mary Knight Halloran, daughter of WAVE sportscaster Joe Knight, remember appearing with Kallay as he talked and introduced cartoons. "I didn't think that much about it," she said. "I suppose I thought everyone's dad and family was on TV. I would also spend hours looking at the sets and props after the shows were off the air, and the 'Funny Flickers' set would get creepy if you were by yourself with Tom Foolery and no Uncle Ed."

Kallay's daughter Kaelin was a full-time host on the show one day when her father had an attack of intestinal flu on the air. "He just ran off and told me to handle things," she said, "so I'm talking with Sylvester, asking him if he knew where Uncle Ed went, just filling time between the cartoons. It made me feel very grown up."

In 1961, another resident came to the Magic Forest—"Miss Julie the Story Lady", aka Julie Shaw. She had already done "Romper Room" shows in Indianapolis and Grand Rapids. "I replaced a cartoon," she said with a laugh. "They paid me $7.50 every time I went on the air and told a story. So the first thing I did was go to J.C. Penney and buy an orange apron with big pockets. I'd put props in the pockets and use them to tell the story. I'd take a toy from my son's toy box for a prop. And I'd really try to remember the stories I'd tell, because at night my kids would ask me to tell them the story I'd told on the air that day, and sometimes I couldn't remember it."

Kallay had his own unique way of introducing Shaw. "He'd say, 'Let's throw it to Miss Julie over on the stump,' and I'd take something out of my pocket and start talking about it."

Kallay also hosted "Guess Who," a Saturday-morning quiz show sponsored by Thornbury's Toys. Joan Combs remembers appearing on it as a seven-year-old. "We all rode in on a fire truck, or got to sit on one, anyway," she said. "We sat on bicycles to answer the quiz questions, about characters from books or nursery rhymes. You would ring bicycle bells to signal an answer. You got Thorny Bucks for points, and then you got to spend them on a big wall of prizes. I picked out a pink plastic Show Boat. (It had little stage sets you could change, and little cardboard figures to move around. It came

To celebrate WAVE-TV's 25th anniversary in 1973, Ed Kallay and Julie Shaw recreated their "Magic Forest" roles as Uncle Ed and Miss Julie the Story Lady. Right: Shaw when she took the role in 1961.

with a book of scripts for scenes you could stage with it, from 'The Wizard of Oz,' 'Tom Sawyer,' and some other shows.) After the game show was over, my mother had to tell them that she had already gotten me a Show Boat for my birthday, and could I please pick a different prize. I got another chance, and picked a Tiny Baby Chatty Cathy. She still talks. I was a celebrity on my block for about three minutes."

By the mid 1960s, however, Kallay's kid-show days had ended. "Magic Forest" went off the air in 1965. Kallay continued broadcasting sports, and Miss Julie the Story Lady went back to being Julie Shaw and continued co-hosting "The Morning Show." Sylvester the Duck still lives at Kaelin Kallay Rybak's home, and looks pretty good for being almost 50.

"Popeye and Lolita"

During his decades with WHAS radio and TV, Sam Gifford left quite a legacy. He was longtime host of "Hi Varieties," program director and active in the Crusade for Children.

Above all, however, he was the brains behind Lolita the Parrot's TV career. "That's the one I should've gotten a Golden Mike Award for," he said with a chuckle.

It happened in 1961. To complement the "T-Bar-V Ranch" show in the mornings, there was a daily afternoon show of cartoons hosted by Randy and Cactus. But something was missing. "The producer said he needed something different for that show," Gifford recalled. "I said, 'Well, why not get a talking parrot?' Everybody thought I was nuts."

Enter Lolita. Her "voice" was actually a sped-up

recording of Randy or studio artist Allan Blankenbaker, depending on who you ask. Despite the name, Lolita was a male, and he had comments on everything from the space race to Mickey Mantle. Once he spoke of attending college, and the University of Louisville obligingly sent a course catalog.

Call him bold, call him irreverent. Those who worked with Lolita called him something else. "What a neurotic parrot," said Milton Metz. "Just nuts. Like that chimp that went wild on the Today Show."

"That godawful bird," recalled Jerry Rice, who worked in the WHAS film department in the early 1960s. "Even if you fed it, it would try to bite your finger off. Sometimes he would get out of his cage and fly around the studio. We'd try to catch it and then think, well, what if we did? He'd bite your hand off!"

Lolita, a parrott who might have benefited from Prozac, co-starred with Randy and Cactus on "Cartoon Circus" in the 1960s.

CHAPTER 4

Kings, Queens and Dancing Fools: The Teen Shows

The opening went like this:

Here we are with Hi Varieties,
ev'ry kind of taste we try to please.
Old songs and new songs,
and gay songs and blue;
dancing as you like it, too.
Get on board for Hi Varieties,
it's the greatest, everyone agrees.
Now your emcee, Sam Gifford,
with talent you know,
Kentuckiana's teenage show!

Then announcer Bill Brittan would chime in:

"This is Hi Varieties, brought to you in part by Frisch's Drive-In Restaurants, and presenting the finest teenage talent in Kentuckiana … now your host and emcee, Sam Gifford!"

Then Gifford, with a smooth, unassuming voice, would do a little banter:

"We have what we think is a fine show for you … some of what we feel is the finest young talent in Kentucky and Southern Indiana. I have a Kleenex with me because we're missing 16 kids from our chorus because of the flu. I don't know if you heard Red Skelton the other night, but he said they're having terrible trouble over in Asia – everybody's got the American flu!"

"Hi Varieties" was a talent show for local teenagers, with music provided by Johnny Schrader.

It was open to anyone who showed up at the station on audition nights. Gifford, the host and David Jones, the director-producer, judged hundreds, even thousands of singers, accordion players, dancers, accordion players, ventriloquists, accordion players, jugglers and accordion players. When they didn't make it, Gifford and Jones would tell them why and invite them to try again. All

Sam Gifford, host of "Hi Varieties," and wife Phyllis Knight, hostess of "Small Talk," doing a broadcast in the late 1950s.

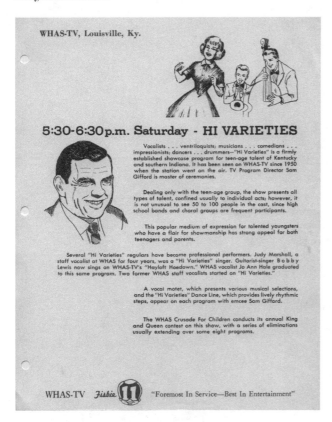

types of music were accepted. In 1965, Gifford told an interviewer, "We have no objection to rock acts so long as the performers look like ladies and gentlemen and they play their music clean and decently."

One group who auditioned was told by Gifford "that we could take them, but first they must cut their hair and change clothes. The parents in the audience applauded. 'We tell them that and they don't listen,' one mother told me. But I tell them and they do it."

Gifford began "Hi Varieties" on WHAS radio and it moved to television as soon as WHAS went on the air, staying in its spot on early Saturday evenings for virtually all of its 20-year-run. Gifford turned over hosting duties to Van Vance in late 1965, but remained active behind the scenes. (He was also longtime program director at WHAS radio and TV.)

"Sam still has people, middle-aged people, come up to him," said his wife, Phyllis Knight. "They'll say hello, and he'll look at them and say, 'You played the piano.' He might not remember their names, but he remembers their talent."

Some performers became semi-regulars on the show, including singers Bob Bowman and Judy Marshall, ventriloquist Lee Dean and the Motet Singers. "It was a great training ground," said Bowman, who went on to a recording career in the early 1960s. "Sam was tough – but what he'd tell you was what you needed to know to succeed."

Into the late 1960s, the WHAS Crusade for Children had a King and Queen who performed at the telethons – usually they'd begun on "Hi Varieties" and made it to their royal posts after several weeks of on-air talent competitions.

The show also ran contests, in conjunction with longtime sponsor Frisch's, designed to make its young viewers better citizens – and active hamburger consumers.

C.D. Kaplan remembers being named "Big Boy of the Week." He and a friend went to the Bowman Field Frisch's "and hit up customers for their ballots. It was how it was done. Then when we had enough we waited until the midnight Sunday deadline to make sure none of our other friends had stuffed the box that week. For the week, I won 14 Big Boys, which I had to eat the week of my reign, and a gift certificate of some sort."

Ike Goen remembers appearing on another local teen talent show – WAVE's "Teen Beat."

"We appeared on the show April 8, 1967," he said. "I was a junior at Salem (Indiana) High School and my band was The Rogues. I was drummer.

Jim Lucas (far right) was a WAVE-TV personality who hosted "Teen Beat" and his own variety show in the 1960s.

We played four songs – 'I Think We're Alone Now' by Tommy James, 'I'm a Believer' and 'I'm Not Your Stepping Stone' by The Monkees and 'Happy Together' by the Turtles. I know our three guitar players were very excited because the amplifiers provided by Tiller & Co. were the same Vox amplifiers used by The Beatles the weekend before at a show in Freedom Hall! We went to WAVE-TV on a Monday evening for the taping of the show, which was played on the air the following Saturday evening."

Bob Kay hosted "Teen Beat" at the beginning, "then they said I was too old to do that, and they hired Jim Lucas." The show's name was eventually changed to "The Jim Lucas Show" before ending its run in 1970.

For a short time, WHAS also began a dance party show. "Teen Time Dance Party," hosted by Jim Walton, ran for a few months in 1958. Walton's daughter Monnie was on hand for at least one of the shows.

"To dance on that show, that was really something," she recalled. "And somebody was chosen at random each week to make a phone call to a star – someone plugging a movie or record. I won one week, and I thought my father was going to fall through the floor. If it hadn't been live, he would have had them do the drawing again."

From the day WLKY began broadcasting on September 23, 1961, a teen dance show was part of the schedule. It began as "TV Jamboree" and then the name was changed to "Dance Party" before it went off the air in the summer of 1963. Al Henderson and Bill Bennett were the show's best-known hosts.

Jerry Rice and his wife Marty appeared on the show as dancers. "The show was sponsored by Ranch House Restaurants, and your friends would have to write letters in to the station to nominate you," said Rice.

Within a few months, Rice was an employee at WLKY and found himself working behind the scenes at "Dance Party."

"They called me in one day because Johnny Tillotson was going to be on the show. They told me I had to run the soundboard, and I'd never done that in my life. I was sweating bullets, but it went all right. It was TV on a shoestring."

The Motet Singers, appearing here on the set of "Hayloft Hoedown", were semi-regulars on "Hi Varieties."

CHAPTER 5

Music Shows, From Crumbling Stagecoaches to Exploding Beer Commercials

They were in prime time, they were locally produced and they were very, very popular.

Throughout most of the 1950s, WHAS's "Hayloft Hoedown" and WAVE's "The Pee Wee King Show" occupied cushy evening time slots. "Hayloft" usually aired on Friday nights alongside such CBS shows as "Topper," "Our Miss Brooks" and "The Twilight Zone." "The Pee Wee King Show" was a regular Thursday night entry with the likes of NBC's "Dragnet" and Groucho Marx's "You Bet Your Life."

Pee Wee King and his band pose with announcer and straight man Bob Kay in the 1950s.

The "Pee Wee King Show" is on the air, brought to you by – as if you couldn't tell – Oertel's '92 Beer.

"The Pee Wee King Show" appeared on the WAVE schedule as early as January 2, 1949, when the station was broadcasting only from 7 to 11 p.m. and was still dark at least one day a week. Joining King was his regular touring band, the Golden West Cowboys, including vocalist Redd Stewart. Announcer Bob Kay was there as commercial spokesman and comic relief.

"Working with Pee Wee was my favorite," Kay said. "We started together in radio and worked so well together. He was a true gentleman."

The show was sponsored by Oertel's '92 beer, and Kay became well-known for his expertise at opening and pouring a cold one on the air, all while talking. But one night someone slipped Kay a hot, shaken-up can. "And when we're doing the commercial, Pee Wee is standing right next to me, in these beautiful, spangled Western garments he used to wear. And I said something like 'See how easy it is to open,' and of course the beer exploded all over myself and him," Kay said.

While the show was on the air, a dispute raged in

Above, King and his band in the early 1950s.

Below, King and his band on WAVE-TV's 25th anniversary show in 1973.

the courts over the authorship of King's most popular song, "Tennessee Waltz," which he co-wrote with Stewart. When recordings of the song by Ernest Tubb and Patti Page became big hits, Tubb claimed authorship of the song because Stewart was under contract to him at the time. The suit was finally settled in King and Stewart's favor in 1951, and the two would collaborate on several other classics, including "Slowpoke."

A story about the settlement appeared in *The Courier-Journal* on June 17th – right next to an article headlined "Randy Atcher To Star In New TV Show" – something called "Hayloft Hoedown."

The "Hayloft Hoedown" gang in 1953: Left to right, Sleepy Marlin, Bea and Mary House, Shorty Chesser, Tiny Thomale, Bernie Smith, George and Janie Workman, and Randy Atcher.

From virtually its first broadcast on June 22, the format and performing family of "Hayloft Hoedown" was in place.

They included Atcher, "Cactus" Tom Brooks, pianist-accordionist Tiny Thomale, guitarists Bernie Smith and Shorty Chesser, fiddler Sleepy Marlin, bassist-banjoist George Workman and singers Janie Workman and the House Sisters, Bea and Mary.

On the first show, the House sisters sang "Chicken Song" and "Mockingbird Hill." Workman sang and yodeled her way through "I'd Love to Be a Cowgirl" and joined Atcher for the show's religious number, "If I Could Hear My Mother Pray." There was square dancing and a gag routine between Randy and Cactus.

For the next twenty years, the theme song was a

weekly standard in households across the city, as from this 1958 airing:

"Come on everybody, all join in the fun,
lots of song and dancing, fun for everyone.
Hear the fiddles ringing, guitars keepin' time,
come on everybody, 'cause it's Hayloft Hoedown time!"

Then announcer Bill Brittan would say:
"Stokley Van Camp, who bring you Stokley's Shellie Beans, the country cooking favorite, presents Hayloft Hoedown, a rollicking half hour of fun and music with Cactus Tom Brooks, the Red River Ramblers, the Sharpe twins, the Hayloft Hoedowners with Stu Shacklett... and now here he is, Kentuckiana's favorite singing cowboy, and the star of the wide open spaces, Randy Atcher!"

The Sharpe twins, Janice and Janette, were vocalists on "Hayloft Hoedown" in the late 1950s.

"At one point, the highest-rated TV program here was Jackie Gleason, and we regularly beat them out," said Bob Pikington, who produced "Hayloft Hoedown" for much of the 1950s and 60s. "A lot of it had to do with Randy Atcher–a big name, a great personality, a good musician. In fact, all those guys were great musicians."

"We were extremely fortunate to have the musicians we had," added Atcher. "None of them were drinkers or people you couldn't depend on. Every rehearsal they were there to do whatever was necessary."

Shorty Chesser, Randy Atcher and Shirley Cardinal sing a number during the 1953 "Hayloft Hoedown" Christmas show.

"We'd try to pace the show, offer something for all musical tastes," said Pilkington. "There'd be a ballad, then an uptempo tune, then an instrumental."

There were even attempts at production numbers. One in particular featured a stagecoach driven by Randy with Shorty Chesser riding shotgun. "We were singing the song 'Deadwood Stage' from 'Calamity Jane' and we'd built this stagecoach out of plywood," Atcher said. "We were sitting atop two pieces of pole and they'd push it back and forth to look like we were riding on it."

In March 1957 "Hayloft Hoedown" had a barn-raising party to celebrate completion of a larger set. Here, Randy Atcher sings...

Calamity occurred when the stagecoach started to slide off one of the poles. Tom Brooks ran backstage to help, "and you could see him on camera crawling around on the floor trying to keep everything from falling apart," Atcher said.

"It was a disaster," Pilkington added. "Randy was supposed to be cracking this bullwhip, only he couldn't really crack it because he was too close to the technicians, so someone backstage had to match his whip cracks. Those got out of synch, and the stagecoach was falling apart, and by the end of the number everyone broke up laughing."

Another time, fiddler Sleepy Marlin appeared on the show to refute news of his own demise. He'd been at a fiddling contest in Canada, and after winning first prize the news was confused with that of a traffic accident.

"Somehow the headlines got crossed up," Marlin said, and there were reports that he had been killed in a car wreck. "I didn't know what had happened until I got back, and the next night was the show. So on the air they asked me about it, and I said, well, I'd been in Canada for this contest, and when I saw the news I had to rush back for my funeral."

...while Tiny Thomale and "Cactus" Tom Brooks clown around in a comedy segment.

There were constants to "Hayloft Hoedown" – one was the ending inspirational number, usually sung by Atcher. "People would request 'The Golden Key' a lot," Atcher said. "And Janie and I would sing 'Whispering Hope.' "

The other constant was the studio audience made up of a troop of Boy or Girl Scouts. Cactus would spend a segment with them where they'd tell jokes and riddles.

"We chose scout troops," Pilkington said, "because that was the easiest place to get an audience."

More regulars came and went, and by the mid-1960s they included singers Sherry Sizemore, Judy Marshall and Jo Ann Hale. Production grew more sophisticated – Pilkington would film Atcher doing a number at the old Seventh Street rail station, or Jo Ann Hale singing "Come Fly with Me" in front of an airplane at Bowman Field.

The show went to videotape, giving the performers the chance to actually watch their own work for a change. Marlin remembers watching an episode on TV in the late 1960s while holding his youngest son.

"He's sitting on my lap," Marlin recalled. "And he looks at the set, and then he looks at me, and then he looks back at the set. He was totally puzzled."

Through it all, the camaraderie remained. Jerry Rice worked in the WHAS film department in the early 1960s and witnessed it firsthand.

"When they were doing the show on Friday nights, they'd do a dress rehearsal and then go down to the cafeteria for dinner," Rice said. "I used to love to be around them. It was family, it was fun. They were a very close-knit group."

At Bowman Field, "Hayloft Hoedown" producer Bob Pilkington works with Jo Ann Hale on "Come Fly With Me," about 1965.

Below: Shorty Chesser and Judy Marshall.

62

Above: The Hayloft Hoedowners perform a square dance—always a popular segment on the show. In the background are Sleepy Marlin, Bernie Smith, and the Motet Singers.

Right: Randy Atcher is backed by Tiny Thomale, Shorty Chesser, George Workman and Bernie Smith.

CHAPTER 6

Uncle Ed

It's May 25, 1973. The Louisville Chamber of Commerce is honoring Muhammad Ali at an award dinner. Ali stands up and says, "You should never forget where you come from. I was just a poor boy here in Louisville who used to ride his bicycle to the gym. The Chamber of Commerce was not behind me then. But Ed Kallay was. Sorry, Mr. Chamber of Commerce, but you're going to have to put on [this award] 'From Muhammad Ali to Mr. Ed Kallay.'"

It's 1969 and the University of Louisville is losing – badly – to Memphis State in a football game. Coach Lee Corso is waving a white towel on the sidelines. The final score will be 69-19. Ed Kallay is calling the game and someone talks about Memphis State's bowl chances.

"Sure, Memphis State belongs in a bowl," says Kallay on the air. "The toilet bowl."

Right: Ed Kallay at ringside with "Tomorrow's Champions" in 1954, a boxing show that helped young Muhammad Ali get his start.

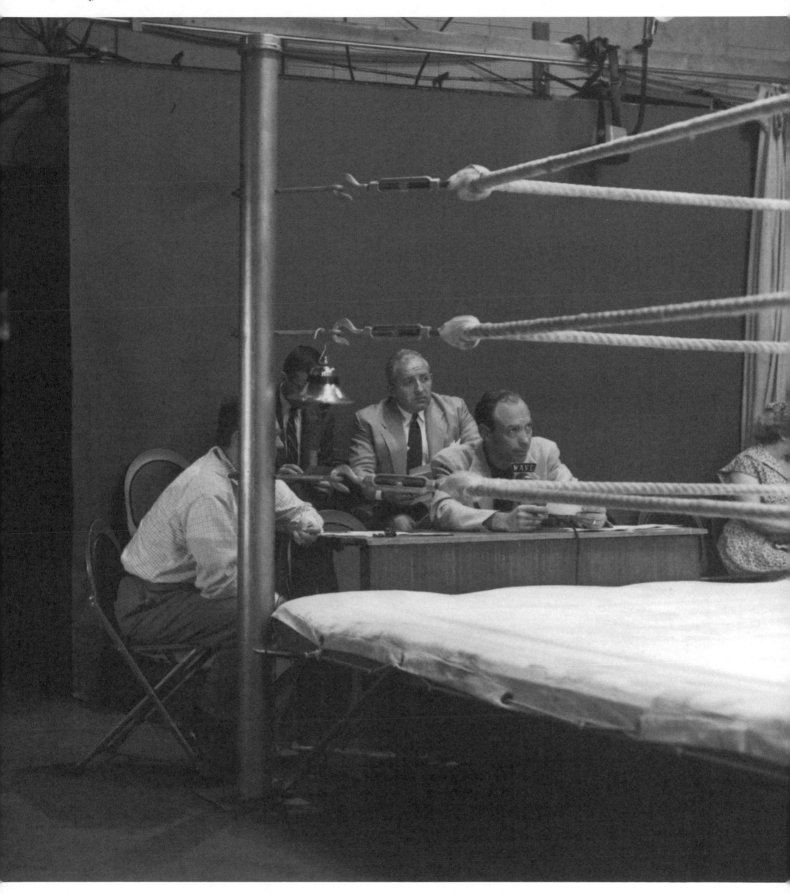

It's a spring evening in 1971. Ed Kallay is doing his 11 p.m. sportscast on WAVE-TV and he introduces a film segment he shot that day at the state basketball championship. He sits. No film. Then it dawns on him.

"Whoops!," he says to Louisville. "This is nobody's fault but my own. I know where that film is. It's lying up on my desk. Tell you what, folks, we'll have it for you later in the show."

Sportscaster, reporter, commentator, kid-show host, commercial pitchman, disk jockey, exercise instructor. Edwin Alexander Kallay was all of those, and above all he was always himself.

In his career at WAVE from 1948-77, Kallay was:

— "Uncle Ed" of the kid show "Funny Flickers."

— The exercise guy on "The Morning Show," teaching sit-ups to housewives.

— The host of the amateur boxing show "Tomorrow's Champions," where Ali first gained wide notice.

— WAVE's sports director and main sports anchor.

— The radio voice of the University of Louisville football and basketball teams, the Kentucky Colonels ABA team and the Louisville Colonels minor-league baseball team.

During a Kentucky Colonels game, Louie Dampier had a foul committed against him. Kallay said to him (and the radio audience), "Hit him back, Louie!"

During a Louisville Colonels baseball game, the umpire called a pitch a ball when Kallay thought it should have been a strike.

"Horse _____!" he said on the air.

No one complained; most people laughed. Years later, Kallay had a phone call one night.

"My wife and I are having an argument," the caller said. "Did you say bull ____, or horse ____?"

Kallay's daughter Kaelin laughs at recalling that story. "Dad just told him what he said, the guy said thanks, and hung up."

"Dad was as real as it came," said Kallay's son Mike, "for better or worse. But there was something so genuine about him, and people responded to that."

A native of Detroit who grew up in Cleveland, Kallay was stationed at Fort Knox briefly during World War II. There he met Louisvillian Mary Jane Cottom, and after the war he came back to marry her. He came back after serving in the 2nd Armored Division in Africa, England and Europe. He had earned a Silver Star and a Purple Heart — after being wounded by a German bullet and leading his company until he became dizzy from a loss of blood.

He returned with less hair — "I like to think it was the helmet," he told an interviewer in 1971. He had a long face that broke into frequent smiles, and smiling eyes that always seemed to be winking. He wasn't telegenic, by any means — he'd often go on TV with half-glasses on the end of his nose.

But he knew his stuff. And he knew when not to take himself too seriously.

Kallay with a lifelong friend, Olympic great Jesse Owens, at a 1973 dinner honoring Kallay and Muhammad Ali.

He'd sometimes switch to a melodramatic tone of voice when reading a story on the air – his way of letting you know that the story wasn't melodramatic at all. He ad-libbed with the best of them, and found his niche in sports. "You can't have any fun with news," he said in 1967. "Everything is too serious."

His broadcasting career began when his mother-in-law told him he had a nice voice and should be on the radio, and he worked at radio station WINN for over two years, joining WAVE in 1948 and doing the first televised commercial when the station went on the air.

In 1950, the family moved from St. Matthews to the West End, wanting more integrated surroundings. The Kallays were a part of the neighborhood for the next forty-five years.

During that time, Kallay traveled with the teams he was covering, taking sons Thomas, Paul and Mike. Daughter Kaelin, the youngest, played the rooster on "Magic Forest" and helped her dad do exercises on "The Morning Show."

"Dad loved working at the station, and we always felt like we were a part of it," she said. "When he was home, he wanted to play with us. I remember one Sunday afternoon when he said, 'That's enough homework! Let's go out and play touch football!' He wanted to enjoy the time he had with us."

"He regards his opinions highly," son Mike wrote in 1969. "He stands ready to defend his position at all times. Among those who often challenge his opinions are members of his family. Discussions range from cordial to 'go to your room.' And when the family outvotes him, he goes to *his* room. … Relaxation is not a part of Kallay's makeup. Work

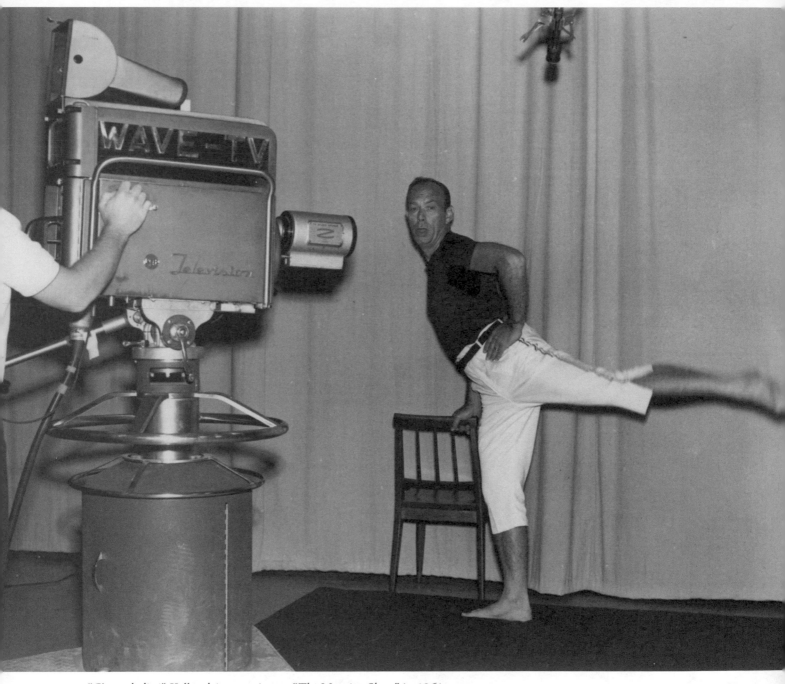

"C'mon, ladies!" Kallay doing exercises on "The Morning Show" in 1961.

is his relaxation. If he worked a 9-to-5 job, he'd have gone out of his mind years ago."

By the mid-1970s, it wasn't enough to be a knowledgeable sportscaster. Some news directors thought you also had to be handsome. When one such specimen came to work at WHAS, Dave Kindred, then sports editor of *The Courier-Journal*, held a

"Most Beautiful Sportscaster" competition. Kallay won in a walk.

But he also knew he'd been in the right place at the right time.

"I remember having a conversation with him in our backyard one afternoon," Mike Kallay said.

"He said if he was starting out in the business today, he'd never have been hired. It was different. Things had changed enormously."

Kallay retained his popularity and his credibility, however. One night, daughter Kaelin recalled, her father was driving home from the station after a late newscast.

"Dad stopped at a stop light and this threatening-looking guy pulls up next to him," she said. "Dad's looking straight ahead, trying not to notice, and the guy says, 'Hey, Kallay! What's the score?' Dad said, 'Oh, everything's fine.' The guy says, 'No! What's the score? He really wanted to know the score of a ball game that night. Dad told him, the guy said thanks and then drove on."

On Saturday morning, April 30, 1977, Kallay did something he'd done hundreds of times over the preceding 27 years. He made a personal appearance – this time at a parade in Clarksville.

On his way home, he stopped at a supermarket to buy milk. There, in the aisle, he collapsed and died of a heart attack. He was 59.

Tributes written afterward recalled the Ali award story, the on-air mugging, the hometown rooting, the "horse___" incident, and others.

At Ratterman's Funeral Home in the West End, thousands of people came to pay their respects to the man with whom they had shared so much.

"I noticed that on the board outside the funeral home they had 'Ed Kallay' spelled out," Mike Kallay said. "I tracked down Tony Ratterman and told him to just put 'Uncle Ed' on there. He was my dad, but he was everyone's uncle."

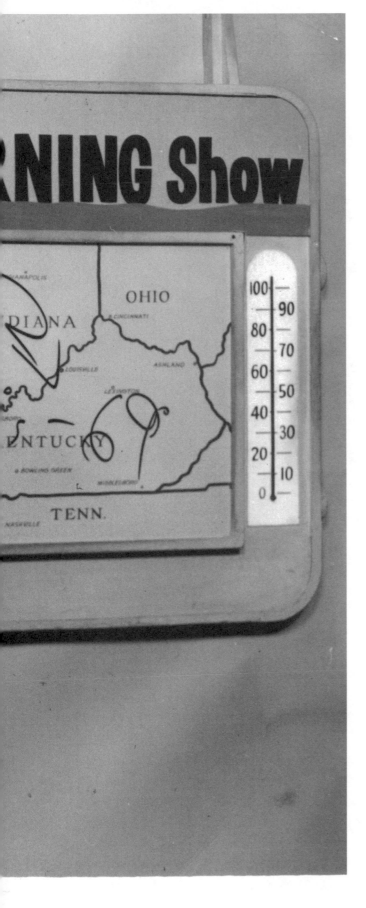

CHAPTER 7

Talk and Public Affairs Shows; Pay No Attention to the Smiling Monkey

Julie Shaw's career at WAVE-TV began with an audition. "George Patterson called me in," said Shaw, who'd already had TV experience in Indianapolis, Evansville and Grand Rapids. "He gave me a loaf of bread and said, 'Here. Sell it.'"

She did.

"Then he asked me, 'How are you in the mornings?' I said, 'I beg your pardon?' He said there were going do to start doing a morning show with Ryan Halloran, and they needed a co-host."

"The Morning Show" was a WAVE staple from 1961 to 1980, hosted for most of its run by Shaw and Halloran. In 1962, it became the first local show to be broadcast in color.

"Ryan and I had 13 years together," Shaw said. "He is a wonderful family man and wonderful to work with. I could start a sentence and he could finish it."

Left: Ryan Halloran doing the weather on "The Morning Show" in 1961. Halloran co-hosted the show from 1961 to 1974.

73

"The idea was simple," Halloran said. "We wanted to make the area look good. We'd have on a child who had done good work in school, or people who had won a ballgame. And we did all the guest bookings ourselves – I think that actually made it better because it gave us more time to talk to them and prepare ourselves."

Then again, some things could not be prepared for. Like the time an inquisitive anteater kept trying to poke its nose up Shaw's skirt. Or the time Baby Opal the elephant heard the call of nature live on the air. Or the time a trained chimp was the guest.

"All of us were sitting in a semi-circle with the chimp and his trainer," Shaw recalled. "And on the monitor I could see that the cameraman had gone in very close on the chimp's face without showing anything else on the screen. And then I saw why – the chimp didn't have on any underwear and he was, shall we say, very, very excited."

Celebrity interviews could be almost as hazardous, and Shaw and Halloran each have their favorites.

With Shaw, it was an encounter with Danny Kaye. It was on a press junket and one crew after another was going in to talk to Kaye and coming out disgusted. He was uncooperative, crude and rude, they said, and they had no usable film footage.

"I was number eight or so on the list and I had to think of something fast," said Shaw. "So I went in and I said, 'Mr. Kaye, let's play a little game. I'm a little girl, lost in an airport. What would you do?

How would you help me?' And he spent four or five minutes doing a little comic bit, soothing me, tying my little shoes. And we got some great, fun footage out of that."

With Halloran, it was an interview with Burt Reynolds, who had just posed for his infamous nude layout in *Cosmopolitan* magazine. He was on the road promoting the film *The Man Who Loved*

Cat Dancing. Everyone had been asking him about the photo layout, and he was getting a little testy.

When Halloran asked him about it, Reynolds cooly referred to a news story from 1937. "You probably think the Hindenburg is still big news," he said. "That was a disaster," Halloran countered. "Are you saying this was a disaster, too?"

Below: As befits a largely female viewing audience, fashion segments were a staple of "The Morning Show," as were clothing commercials done by co-host Julie Shaw (opposite page). But by the late 1960s, discussions of current issues and the controversies of the day were included on the show as well.

Phyllis Knight and Randy Atcher at a WHAS Crusade for Children telethon in the late 1950s.

Phyllis Knight and "Small Talk"

As hostess of the WHAS series "Small Talk" from 1956-1969, Phyllis Knight did her share of celebrity interviews – everyone from Eleanor Roosevelt to Trigger.

"Roy Rogers came on the show," Knight said, "and he said if you pat Trigger in a certain spot on his head, he'd bow. So when the time came to sign off, I said, 'Good night, Trigger,' but I patted him a little higher than I should have, and he started going toward the camera! And I was saying, 'Whoa, Trigger! Whoa!'"

"Small Talk" was a part of the WHAS nightly newscast, all of which took place in one studio.

"So you'd have to get your guests out quietly while the news was on, because they'd be right next to you," Knight said.

And there was always talent on hand in case a guest didn't show up. "You could always turn to Cactus and Randy," Knight said. "And Milton Metz was always good to talk with."

As the cultural shockwaves of the later 1960s were felt in Louisville, Knight began doing shows on

Phyllis Knight interviewing former first lady Eleanor Roosevelt in the mid-1950s.

On "Small Talk" Phyllis Knight interviewed everyone from future president Ronald Reagan...

more controversial topics. She spent a week in Eastern Kentucky to do a report on the first doctor in the area to give birth control pills.

"With something like that, expense was a secondary concern," she said. "The first concern was to inform our audience, to tell the story."

There were also shows on sex education and race relations. "We did an hour show in sex education

in the schools when they began that," Knight recalled. "We used words like penis and vagina. I had a bandage on my hand at that time because of tendonitis, and some minister from Indiana called and said they should have put that bandage on my mouth. There were people out there who just despised me for reporting this kind of thing."

On another show, Knight was interviewing some Afro-American leaders when one of them, an off-camera friend, used Knight's first name. "The phones lit up," Knight recalled. "But I'm grateful that I had some credibility, that people trusted me. I used that as much as I could. I went to speak to the Louisville Rotary Club in the 1960s and talked to the men there about their wives and the risk of cervical cancer. We spread the word about pap smears, and helped clear up some misconceptions about adoption that led to a big increase locally."

For her work, Knight won Golden Mike awards from *McCall's* magazine in 1958 and 1963 as the outstanding woman broadcaster in America.

Through it all, there was still time for frivolity. During the station's Kentucky Derby broadcasts in the 1960s and '70s, Knight became known for the fashionable hats she wore during each segment. And she was executive director of the WHAS Crusade for Children from 1975 to 1981 when she helped usher in the annual telethon's first million-dollar year.

...to "Perry Mason" star Raymond Burr.

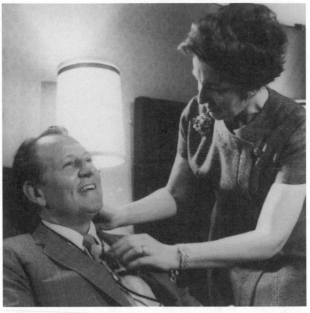

There were always interesting guests on "Small Talk." Above, "Gilligan's Island" star Alan Hale.

Phyllis Knight adjusting the microphone of television icon Art Linkletter.

A made-for-TV film about cancer featuring Knight also played at a local movie theater. Opposite: Phyllis working the Derby.

The Crusade for Children

Since 1954, over five decades and through several sales of WHAS-TV, the Crusade for Children has survived. The telethon has raised tens of millions of dollars to benefit mentally and physically handicapped children, much of it collected by tireless firefighters at hundreds of road intersections.

And everyone has their favorite Crusade stories – like the time one-legged tap dancer Peg Leg Bates lost his airline ticket back to New York. "So he went to the airport and told them about it," Knight said, "and they said, 'Can you prove you're Peg Leg Bates?'"

McLean Stevenson of "M*A*S*H" decided to pole-vault across the orchestra pit at Memorial Auditorium during one Crusade. He didn't make it. And Mel Torme was a little miffed when he came to the Crusade in the 1950s and found that Randy Atcher had better billing than he did.

Celebrities aside, the local performers were and are the ones who make the Crusade tick, and the community loves them for it. When longtime Crusade producer-emcee Jim Walton died in 1985, his funeral procession included dozens of fire trucks from local volunteer divisions.

WAVE had its own telethon, "Bids for Kids," for several years in the 1950s. When the station opened its new studios in 1959, the Norton family celebrated the occasion by commissioning an opera, "Beatrice," to be performed by the Kentucky Opera Association live on the air that fall.

Another WAVE tradition in the late 1950s and early 60s was an annual Christmas special that took up a whole studio, featuring a village set, employees and their children as carolers and Bob Kay as an old toymaker.

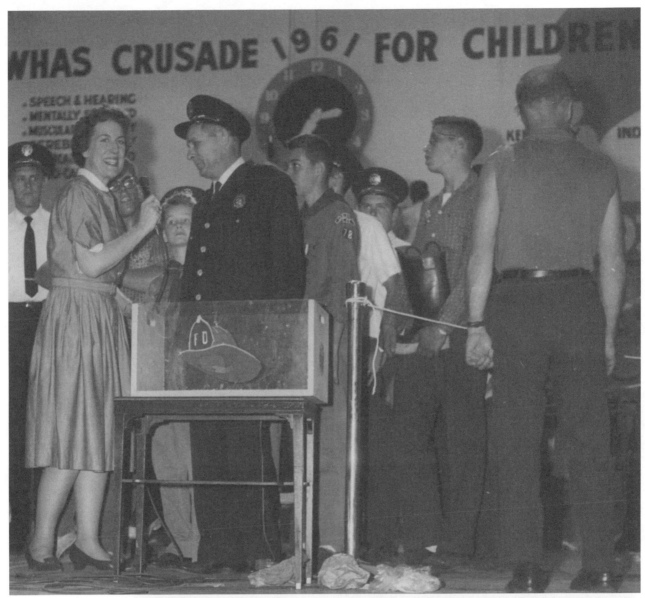

Opposite page: For many years the Crusade for Children was held in Memorial Auditorium.

Above: Phyllis Knight at the 1961 Crusade.

Right: The WAVE-TV Christmas special in 1966.

The End of the Beginning

In the spring of 1969, WAVE began running NBC's "Laugh-In" opposite WHAS's "Hayloft Hoedown" on Saturday nights.

You couldn't ask for a clearer contrast – it was square dancing versus go-go dancing, Randy and Cactus versus Rowan and Martin, gospel music versus Goldie Hawn.

The audience – particularly younger viewers – turned to "Laugh-In." And for the first time in almost twenty years, "Hayloft Hoedown" began fading in popularity.

"We'd start hearing things about how much the show cost to put on each week," co-host Randy Atcher said. "And the station was running some music shows produced in Nashville at the same time that were cheaper. We just concentrated on doing a good show, but you had to wonder what was going to happen."

"All the film syndicates in Hollywood and New York would try to sell you packages," added Jerry Rice, who worked in the WHAS film department in the early 1960s. "It didn't take a genius to figure out you could fill a half-hour or an hour with re-runs of 'Perry Mason' or 'Maverick' instead of a show it cost you to produce."

"It was getting so you could send a show by satellite anywhere in the country," added "Hayloft Hoedown" producer Bob Pilkington, "and a lot of people could fill the time a lot cheaper."

Then in June 1970, one shoe fell – "T-Bar-V Ranch" went off the air, abruptly canceled after more than 20 years. The same problems were cited – expense, lower ratings. At a time when WHAS had shelved "Fisbie" and was advertising itself as "New Look Eleven," shows like "T-Bar-V" seemed, well, quaint.

There were promises of announcing work and a future at WHAS for Atcher and Brooks, but all they had left was "Hayloft Hoedown." And it was cancelled in January 1971. That March, Atcher, 52, and Brooks, 61, were let go.

"I think it just about broke Randy's heart," said Rice.

Atcher went on to perform on a short-lived show called "Hoedown" on WLKY. He got his real-estate license, and also worked religiously recording books at the American Foundation for the Blind. He still performs regularly.

Brooks spent his post-retirement years working at a Louisville liquor store, selling beer and saying "Howdee" to many men and women who had once appeared on "T-Bar-V."

At about the same time, "Small Talk" came to the end of its run after 16 years.

"It was devastating to have something like that pulled out from under you," said Phyllis Knight.

Over at WAVE, there were changes afoot at "The Morning Show." It was determined that Ryan Halloran was appealing enough to younger viewers, and he left in 1974, becoming a co-host of the early morning "Today in Louisville," later "Today in WAVE Country."

Julie Shaw missed her old partner. And the segments she'd been doing about teenage, drug and race issues had resulted in death and kidnapping threats called into the station. "I lost my oomph," she said. "I was scared for me, my family, the whole nine yards."

In 1976, after 15 years, Shaw left "The Morning Show." She had never worked under a contract at WAVE, but had given full-time attention to her job as well as to making hundreds of personal appearances on behalf of the station.

"Those were the days when women didn't expect things like contracts," Shaw said. "I had no retirement, nothing, after all those years." She went to work for the Kentucky State Fair Board before retiring to Florida, but the way she was treated by WAVE still leaves a bad taste in her mouth.

"They started me out at $65 a week, and 15 years later I was getting $125," she said. "I did commercials all over town, wrote copy for clients, did everything to earn a little extra money."

Meanwhile, at WHAS, Phyllis Knight was having a hard time coping. She was forced to work in what she called "the pig pen newsroom." The adjustment was so difficult that she suffered a mental breakdown attributed to depression and menopause issues and was hospitalized for seven weeks in 1975.

Once she recovered, however, she turned the experience into something positive – an award-winning six-part series on depression that aired on WHAS news. And she became executive director of the WHAS Crusade for Children before leaving the station in 1981.

By then, local stations were confining their local programming to news. "That's what they felt they had to offer," said Bob Pilkington. "Local news was what could set them apart from the networks."

"So much of what we did is now done by the weathercasters," added Ryan Halloran.

Today it's unheard of to imagine a TV station celebrating its new building by commissioning an opera. Or by investing money in a program where kids get to celebrate their birthdays by going on TV and waving at their family members, or creating a Magic Forest and puppet characters without trying to sell the merchandising, movie and video-game rights.

But it happened once upon a time – a time when at least a few of television's larger-than-life heroes and heroines lived in our community. Memories of Randy, Cactus, Uncle Ed, Bob Kay, Ray Shelton, Livingston Gilbert, Ryan Halloran, Milton Metz, Phyllis Knight and so many others live on long after their broadcasts – memories of another time, and another way of life, in what now seems like another city.

There have been tributes since then – in 1973 and again in 1993 when WAVE celebrated its heritage, and in the late 1980s when WHAS's "Louisville Tonight" spent a week looking back. To wish that time stood still, and that those days were still with us, is unrealistic and a bit maudlin. But it's nice to reminisce now and then and remember what we watched and who we were.

And there's no denying that the song written and performed by our own Randy Atcher has a permanent place in the collective memory of a whole generation...*Brush your teeth each morning, get lots of sleep at night, mind your mom and daddy...*

Where Are They Now?

Bud Abbott (shown here with Spike Jones) left WHAS in 1956, after 13 years with the station, to join Radio Free Europe. He later settled in North Carolina.

"Cactus" Tom Brooks was with WHAS from 1944 to 1971. From 1950 to 1971 he played Cactus on "T-Bar-V Ranch" and "Hayloft Hoedown." After taking early retirement and leaving WHAS in 1971, Brooks worked in a liquor store, serving quite a few of his now-grown fans. He died in 1997.

Randy Atcher was with WHAS from 1950 to 1971. He still performs locally and regionally and has been a longtime reader for the audio books program at the American Printing House for the Blind.

Foster Brooks, left, and Ryan Halloran emcee the game show "Go For Cash" in 1954.

Foster Brooks, Tom's brother, left Louisville in 1957 for a station in Rochester, N.Y. after stints at WKLO, WAVE and WHAS. In 1962 he left Rochester for Hollywood and played bit parts on various TV shows. In the late 1960s he developed a comic drunk act, which he played to great success at charity golf tournaments. At one tournament his performance caught the eye of Perry Como, and with the support of Como, Bill Cosby and Dean Martin, Brooks became a regular guest on talk and variety shows for most of the 1970s and early 1980s.

Pete French was with WHAS from 1943 to 1957 and was the station's TV newscaster from 1950 to 1957. He was also a newscaster with WLKY in 1962. He died in 1977.

Bob Kay was with WAVE-TV from 1941 to 1982. He is retired and living in Louisville.

Livingston Gilbert was with WAVE for over forty years, from 1939 to 1980, and was the station's main TV newscaster from 1948 to 1980. He died in 1981.

Ed Kallay joined WAVE in 1948 after a stint at WKLO. He stayed with the station as its sports director and main sportscaster until his death in 1977.

Bill Gladden was with WAVE from 1947 to 1971, when he left the station to join Greater Louisville First Federal Savings and Loan. He died in 1975.

Herb Koch was with WHAS from 1933 to 1956, leaving the station to become an organ teacher. He died in 1986.

Joe Knight was a sportscaster and announcer with WAVE from 1955 to 1981 and for WHAS briefly thereafter. He died in 1985.

Milton Metz joined WHAS in 1946 and still does commentaries and commercials for WHAS radio. His call-in radio show, "Metz Here," ran from 1959 to 1993.

Bill Pickett was a vocalist with WHAS from 1946 to 1958. He died in 1995.

Art Metzler was an announcer, producer and sportscaster with WAVE from 1959-88. He died in 2000.

Omer "Shorty" Chesser was a musician on WHAS from 1950 to 1971.

Carl R. "Tiny" Thomale was a staff musician, playing piano and accordion for WHAS from 1950 to 1971. He died in 1993.

Bernie Smith left WHAS in 1967 for the west coast after 29 years, but later returned to Louisville and became mayor of fifth-class city Minor Lane Heights.

Sam Gifford was with WHAS from 1948 to 1987 as announcer, program director and in sales management. He lives with his wife, Phyllis Knight.

Ray Shelton was with WHAS from 1950 to 1975, leaving to join Greater Louisville First Federal Savings and Loan. He did radio and TV spots for the bank from 1950 through the mid-1990s.

Jim Walton was with WHAS from 1939 to 1979, and was emcee of the Crusade for Children from 1953 to 79. He died in 1985, and his funeral procession included volunteer firefighters from all over Kentuckiana.

Pee Wee King had music and variety shows on WAVE-TV as well as on national networks, and was a longtime member of the Grand Ole Opry. He died in 2000.

Phyllis Knight left WHAS in 1981 after 26 years and now lives in retirement with her husband, Sam Gifford.

Julie Shaw left WAVE in 1976 and went to work for the Kentucky Fair Board. She now lives in Florida.

The Shows and When They Ran

According to the Law – Panel/talk show featuring local attorneys, hosted by Ray Shelton: WHAS, November 7, 1954-August 5, 1956.

Bids for Kids – Childrens' telethon: WAVE, 1956-59.

The Boyd Bennett Show – Musical program: WHAS, June 29-July 13, 1953; WAVE, August 5, 1953-September 6, 1954; WLKY, September 25, 1961-September 7, 1962.

Broadway at Midday (Midday Roundup) – News/music program with Jim Walton, organist Johnny Schrader, pianist Tiny Thomale, guitarist Bernie Smith and singer Judy Marshall: WHAS, February 8, 1954-February 5, 1960.

The Bud Abbott Show – Talk/comedy program: WHAS, March 27, 1950-November 20, 1952.

Burley Birch Bark – Homespun humor and music with Rodney Ford as Burley: WAVE, August 31, 1953-January 10, 1955.

Cartoon Circus (Cactus Cartoon Club, Randy and Lolita, Popeye's Cartoon Circus) – Afternoon cartoons featuring "Cactus" Tom Brooks and/or Randy Atcher, with Lolita the Parrot: WHAS, September 26, 1955-September 6, 1968.

Dance Party (TV Jamboree) – Teen dance program hosted by Al Henderson and later Bill Bennett: WLKY, September 23, 1961-July 27, 1963.

Dialing for Discs (Platters & Pix) – Disk jockey show hosted by Ryan Halloran: WAVE, August 1, 1952-October 1, 1954.

Dollar Derby – Game show sponsored by UBC Food Stores: WAVE, June 8, 1951-October 22, 1954.

Donaldson Play Club – Childrens' show sponsored by Donaldson Bread, hosted by Bob Kay: WAVE, June 16, 1953-June 9, 1955.

Flavor to Taste – Cooking show: WAVE, August 11, 1949-August 13, 1954.

The Foster Brooks Show – Music and comedy program: WAVE, September 19, 1950-April 27, 1951.

Funny Flickers (Magic Forest) – Children's program with cartoons, hosted by Ed Kallay and featuring Julie Shaw as Miss Julie the Story Lady (1961-65): WAVE, June 29, 1953-February 12, 1965.

Go for Cash – Game show: WAVE, April 7, 1954-April 22, 1955.

Good Living – Homemaking show hosted by Sam and Marian Gifford (1950-55) and Jean Phair (1955-57): WHAS, March 27, 1950-October 11, 1957.

Guess Who – Saturday morning game show sponsored by Thornbury's Toys, hosted by Ed Kallay: WAVE, May 13, 1961-December 22, 1962; April 13-December 21, 1963; March 21-December 12, 1964.

Guest Book – Talk/interview show hosted by Roz Marquis: WHAS, March 27, 1950-November 8, 1951.

Hayloft Hoedown – Weekly music show featuring Randy Atcher, "Cactus" Tom Brooks, guitarist Bernie Smith, pianist Tiny Thomale, bassist Shorty Chesser, fiddler Sleepy Marlin, singers Janice and Janette Sharpe, George and Janie Workman and others: WHAS, June 22, 1951-January 2, 1971.

Healthy, Wealthy and Wise – Saturday children's show hosted by Ryan Halloran: WAVE, March 10, 1951-April 7, 1956.

The Herbie Koch Show – Music show featuring organist Koch and vocalist Bill Pickett: WHAS, March 30, 1950-June 17, 1956.

Hi-Varieties (Here's Now) – Local teenage talent program hosted by Sam Gifford (1950-65) and Van Vance (1965-71), assisted by organist Johnny Schrader: WHAS, March 27, 1950-mid 1971.

Junior's Club – Children's program hosted by Ed Kallay and featuring ventriloquist Norma Jarboe and her dummy Junior: WAVE, November 27, 1948-September 6, 1950.

Magic Forest – See Funny Flickers.

Man on the Street – Free-wheeling talk/interview show hosted by Foster Brooks: April 30, 1952-August 4, 1953.

Midday Roundup – See Broadway at Midday.

The Morning Show – Daily talk/interview show hosted by, among others, Julie Shaw (1961-76), Ryan Halloran (1961-74) and Dale Greer (1974-77): WAVE, July 31, 1961-March 28, 1980.

The Old Sheriff – Children's show hosted by Foster Brooks: WAVE, April 5, 1950-September 25, 1953.

Pee Wee King Bandstand – Music with King and his band, featuring Redd Stewart: WAVE, December 26, 1957-April 2, 1959.

Pee Wee King Show – Music with King and his band, with comic relief from announcer/ sidekick Bob Kay: WAVE, December 20, 1948-November 25, 1954.

Pop the Question – Game show co-hosted by Bob Kay and Rosemary Reddens, sponsored by Triangle Food Stores: WAVE, January 23, 1951-October 19, 1954.

The Redd Stewart Show – Music show with Gene Engles on piano and Lester Cobb on bass: WAVE, June 17-September 9, 1957.

Renfro Valley Folks – Music show: WAVE, October 28, 1956-April 21, 1957.

Small Talk – Interview program moderated by Mary Snow Ethridge (1951-56) and Phyllis Knight (1956-69): WHAS, January 12, 1951-1969.

Songs of Faith – WHAS, March 10, 1951-July 30, 1967.

Square Dance – WHAS, April 4, 1950-February 9, 1951.

Speculation – Game show based on the stock market, hosted by Bob Kay: WAVE, February 15, 1965-July 8, 1966.

T-Bar-V Ranch – Children's show co-hosted by Randy Atcher and "Cactus" Tom Brooks: WHAS, March 27, 1950-June 26, 1970.

Teen Beat (The Jim Lucas Show) – Teen talent/ dance show later turned into a variety show featuring Lucas: WAVE, February 6, 1965-February 7, 1970.

Teen Time Dance Party – Teen dance show hosted by Jim Walton: WHAS, January 8-May 21, 1958.

Tomorrow's Champions – Program featuring young local boxing talent, hosted by Ed Kallay: WAVE, July 2, 1954-December 11, 1965.

Walton Calling – Music, comedy and audience stunts with Jim Walton, announcer Ray Shelton and organist Johnny Schrader: WHAS, March 29, 1950-February 7, 1955.

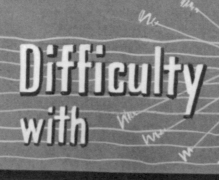